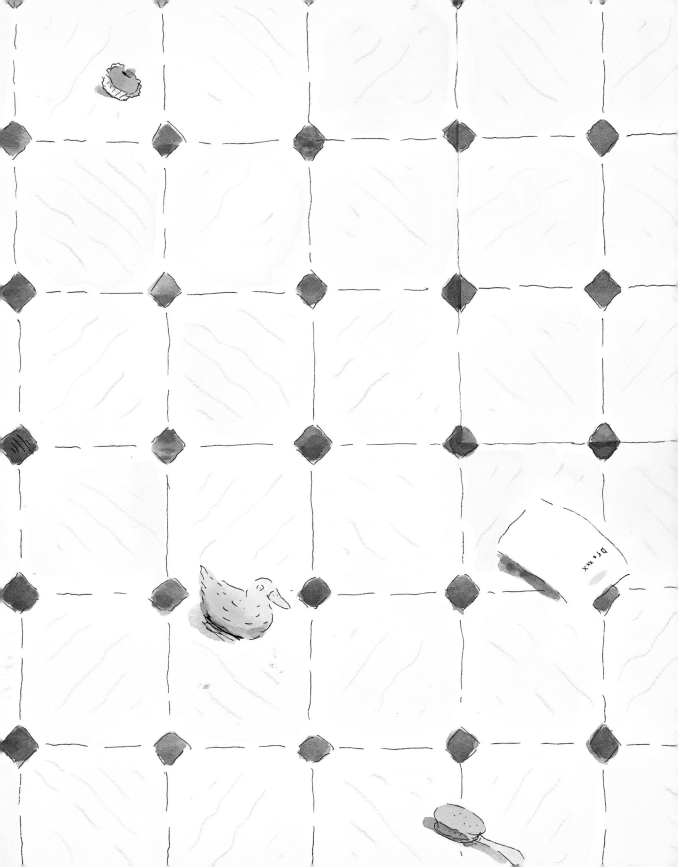

*For Chlöe and Theo*

Tom's Cat
Copyright © 1986 by Charlotte Voake
Published in England by Walker Books Ltd., London
Printed in Italy. All rights reserved.
First Harper Trophy edition, 1986.
Published in hardcover by J. B. Lippincott, New York.

Library of Congress Cataloging in Publication Data
Voake, Charlotte.
  Tom's cat.

  Summary: All the sounds Tom normally hears in his
house become suspicious when his cat is missing.
  [1. Cats—Fiction] I. Title.
PZ7.V855To 1986b      [E]        85-23904
ISBN 0-397-32195-3 (lib. bdg.)

  "A Harper trophy book."
ISBN 0-06-443105-3 (pbk.)        85-27166

# TOM'S CAT

## Charlotte Voake

A Harper Trophy Book

*Harper & Row, Publishers*

# Here is Tom

# looking for his cat.

# CLICK CLICK CLICK

Is that Tom's cat

walking across the floor?

No.

It's Grandma

knitting socks.

click click click

# TAP TAP TAP

Is that Tom's cat
dancing on the table?

# No.

Tom's mother is typing
a letter to a friend.

# SPLASH SPLASH SPLASH

Is that Tom's cat?

No. Cats hate water.

So does Tom's brother.
But here he is,
trying to wash his hair.

CLATTER

CLATTER

CLATTER

What's that?

Is that Tom's cat
bringing everyone
a cup of tea?

No.

That's Tom's dad...

# making pancakes.

And what's this loud noise?

VROOM

VROOM

VROOM

It sounds a bit like

Tom's cat on a ...

# MOTORCYCLE!

VROOM
VROOM

But it's not.

It's Tom's sister

quickly cleaning the carpet

before anyone sees

she's dropped the cake

on the floor.

# So where is Tom's cat?

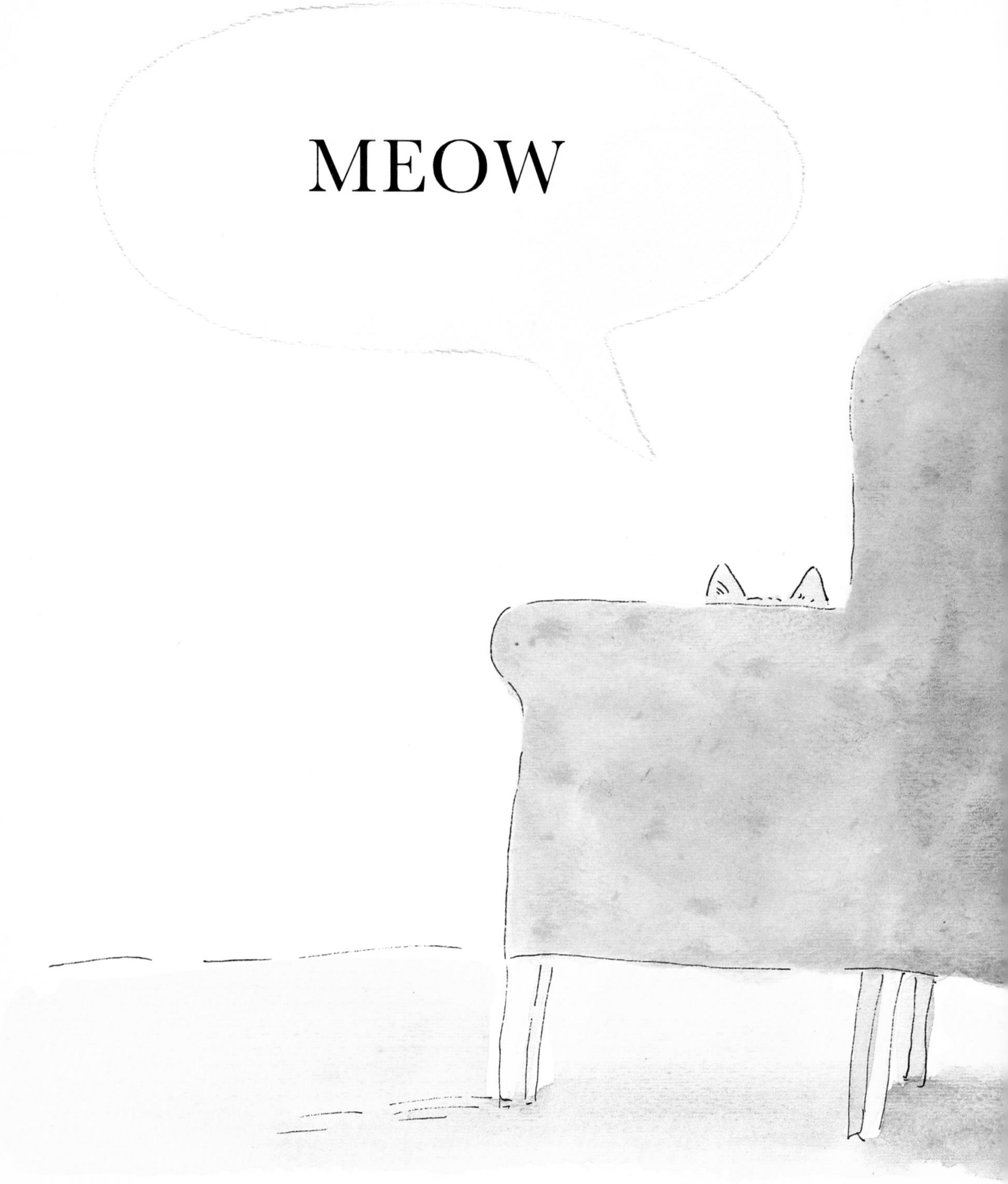
MEOW

That's Tom's cat.

Hello, cat!